To my parents, for giving me roots and wings.

To Brian, Rose, and Perry—my American Dream
is complete with you in it. *Grá go deo.*

To all those striving for their American Dream,
and to the immigration lawyers, advocates,
and activists helping them.

To my brother, Ray; our brilliant team at McEntee Law;
and all our wonderful clients—this book is for you!

www.mascotbooks.com

For more information, please contact:
Mascot Books
620 Herndon Parkway #320
Herndon, VA 20170
info@mascotbooks.com

Library of Congress Control Number: 2019912136

CPSIA Code: PRT0919A
ISBN-13: 978-1-64543-018-6

Printed in the United States

OUR AMERICAN DREAM

Written by Fiona McEntee   Illustrated by Srimalie Bassani

In a country so great with mountains so tall,
was born a dream for one and for all.
That dream is known throughout the land.
The American Dream, a dream so grand!

Immigrants come from countries far,
to dream their dreams beneath American stars.
Let's see who's here in this great place,
what dreams we share in the United States.

Aya's American Dream
began in Syria.
As a child, a refugee,
she came to America.
Now she's in Congress,
wearing her hijab proudly.
She fights for equal rights and
promotes them loudly.

Our friend Rosita is a passionate teacher.
Her dream is big, so she's known as a Dreamer.
Came here as a baby, her family works hard.
They dream together, and dream of getting green cards.

Antonio moved here because he was born this way.
He and Bob celebrate "love is love" on their wedding day.
Their American Dream is for equal rights,
to love one another without judgment or strife.

You also know our neighbors, Perry and Sadie.
They dreamed a dream of a miracle baby.
That baby was born in a country far away.
Once Faith was adopted, with her family she'd stay.

Meet Yulia from Russia. She is an artist extraordinaire!
Her dream is to have her paintings shared.
With the freedom to paint without any troubles,
her American Dream has ended her struggles.

Karima loves computers, a girl born to code.
Her American Dream is a sight to behold.
She moved here for college, decided to stay.
She started a tech company; as a boss lady she slays!

Juma from Tanzania plays soccer all day.
He dreams of America at night when he prays.
Just given the chance,
what might those dreams become?
He could captain the United States
in World Cups to come.

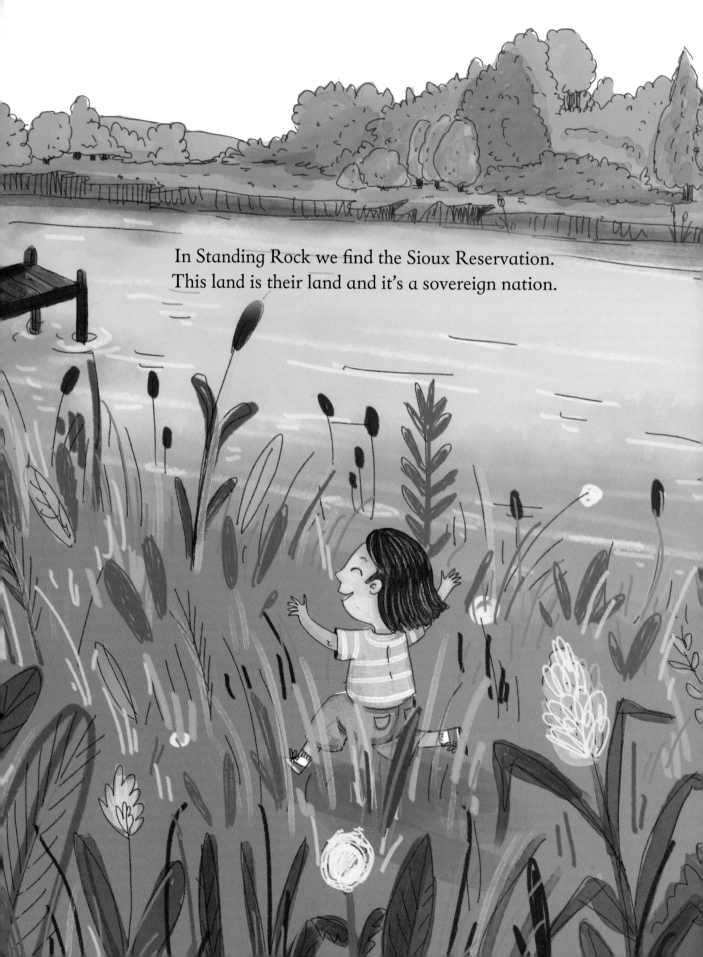

In Standing Rock we find the Sioux Reservation.
This land is their land and it's a sovereign nation.

They work to keep their land protected, their water clean.
Sacred land such as theirs should be more than just a dream.

Some people were forced here, didn't come by choice.
They have since battled for freedom, and used their voice.
We must all be aware, these torments run deep.
And sadly, some dreams are rooted in grief.

Families travel far, by day and by night.
Fleeing terror and violence, it's a dangerous plight.
They seek shelter and refuge at America's door,
like generations of immigrants who have come before.

There are many people in this land of hope and dreams.
United and strong, as the Lady of Liberty beams.

We look not to build walls but to make tables longer.
We gather side by side, because diversity makes us stronger!

We hope you've enjoyed our American Dream.
We've heard countless stories, not so different they seem.
Now it's your turn, what will your hope be?
Are you ready? Let's dream: one...two...three!

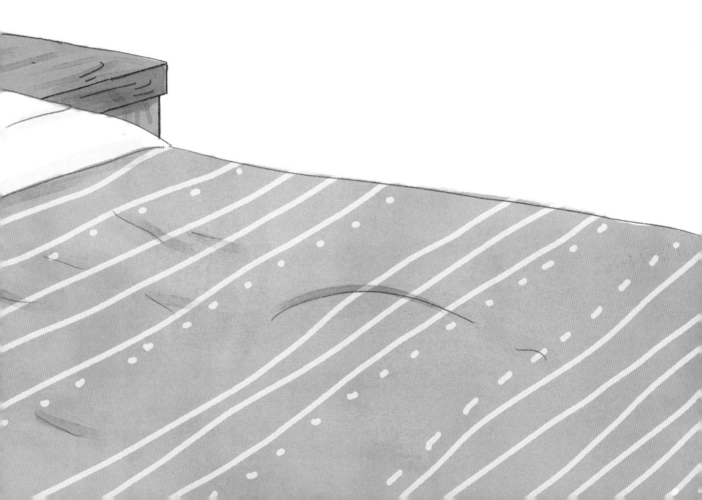

ABOUT THE AUTHOR

Photograph by Owen Farrell

Fiona McEntee is an award-winning, nationally recognized immigration lawyer. She is the founding and managing attorney of McEntee Law Group, an immigration law firm based in Chicago. Fiona and her team of passionate advocates represent individuals and families, as well as some of the world's leading musicians, artists, athletes, innovative entrepreneurs, and multinational and U.S. companies.

Fiona is a national spokesperson for the American Immigration Lawyers Association (AILA). You may recognize her from her frequent national and international media appearances, including on MSNBC, BBC, CNN.com, and RTÉ, and in *Politico*, *The Chicago Tribune*, *The New York Times*, and *Irish Central*, among others.

As a proud Irish immigrant and naturalized U.S. citizen, Fiona has dedicated her career to the advancement of immigrants' rights. As a fearless immigration lawyer, Fiona's efforts range from lobbying in Washington, D.C., to suing the Trump Administration pro bono over the controversial Travel Ban. Fiona has vowed to zealously advocate for immigrant children and parents who face innumerable obstacles as they strive for their American Dream.

Fiona was recently inducted into the Irish American Hall of Fame in the Irish American Heritage Center in Chicago. Some of her other accolades include receiving the ISBA Elmer Gertz Award for her service in advancing and safeguarding human rights, receiving the Chicago-Kent College of Law Outstanding Pro Bono Service Award on behalf of the O'Hare Airport Attorneys (Travel Ban), and being named one of Chicago's Notable Women Lawyers by Crain's Custom Media.

Fiona is an extremely proud mom to Rose and Perry. She is so grateful to her husband, Brian, for his unending love, support, and partnership. They live in Chicago's Lakeview neighborhood and enjoy traveling back to Dublin, Ireland, to visit family and friends.

A PORTION OF THE PROCEEDS FROM
OUR AMERICAN DREAM WILL BE DONATED TO:

- The *I Stand With Immigrants* Initiative, powered by FWD.us Education Fund. As part of this initiative, the *I Am An Immigrant* campaign showcases stories of immigrants and immigration. Together, the campaigns empower immigrants and their allies to share stories and drive action that demonstrate immigration is good for our communities, economy, and country.

- The American Immigration Council, which works to strengthen America by shaping how America thinks about and acts toward immigrants and immigration. The Council brings together problem solvers and employs four coordinated approaches to advance change—litigation, research, legislative and administrative advocacy, and communications. It envisions an America that values fairness and justice for immigrants and advances a prosperous future for all.

A NOTE FROM FIONA

As an immigrant, immigration lawyer, and mom of two young children, I wrote *Our American Dream* to help explain the importance of a diverse and welcoming America. *Our American Dream* highlights different immigrant stories and is inspired by my real-life clients, family, and friends. Thank you so much for trusting me to share your stories.

I truly believe in the American Dream. While everyone's version of that dream is different, we are united in striving for the opportunity to achieve it.

I am eternally grateful to my village of supporters, including my inspirational immigration lawyer colleagues; George, Belle, and the AILA Media Team; my wonderful friends including the LawMamas; and my mentors over the years, especially Irish Senator Billy Lawless.

I'm so humbled to stand beside fierce advocates including the Dreamers such as Belén Sisa, The Young Center for Immigrant Children's Rights, KIND, United We Dream, Undocumented Students for Education Equity at ASU, ACLU, AILA, AIC, IJC, ICIRR, NIJC, NILC, RAICES, Al Otro Lado, BAJI, CAIR-Chicago, AAJC, FWD.us, Immigration Equality, Equality Illinois, Irish Community Services, Irish Stand, Families Belong Together, Puente Human Rights Movement, Cosecha, Define American, Together Rising, Standing Rock Sioux Tribe, Interfaith Community for Detained Immigrants, Vote Mama, Lawyers for Good Government, and Lawyer Moms of America. Thank you also to Senator Durbin and former Congressman Gutiérrez for championing immigrant rights in Congress for so many years.

I would also like to thank Nina and everyone at Mascot Books, and of course Srimalie for sharing her wonderful talent with us and bringing my vision to life.

I'd also like to thank my cousin, Owen, in Ireland for taking my author photo and for the constant encouragement.

Finally, I want to thank my parents for teaching me the value of hard work, generosity, and perseverance.

Go raibh míle maith agaibh!